Library of Congress Cataloging-in-Publication Data
Names: Coxe, Molly, author, illustrator.
Title: Wet hen / by Molly Coxe.
Description: First Kane Press edition. | New York : Kane Press, [2018] |
Series: Bright Owl Books | Summary: "Hen and her eggs keep getting wet but luckily she has a friend who helps her with the rain in this short 'e' sound easy-to-read book"— Provided by publisher.
Identifiers: LCCN 2018000239 (print) | LCCN 2017054183 (ebook) | ISBN 9781575659770 (ebook) | ISBN 9781575659763 (pbk) | ISBN 9781575659756 (reinforced library binding)
Subjects: | CYAC: Rain and rainfall—Fiction. | Chickens—Fiction. | Eggs—Fiction. | Animals—Fiction.
Classification: LCC PZ7.C839424 (print) | LCC PZ7.C839424 Wet 2018 (ebook) | DDC [E]—dc23
LC record available at https://lccn.loc.gov/2018000239

10 9 8 7 6 5 4 3 2 1

Printed in China

Book Design: Michelle Martinez

Bright Owl Books is a
trademark of Kane Press, Inc.

Follow us on Twitter
@KanePress

Visit us online at
www.kanepress.com

Like us on Facebook
facebook.com/kanepress

Wet Hen

by Molly Coxe

Kane Press · New York

Hen is wet.
Hen's eggs are wet.
"Help!" says Hen.

"I can help,"
says Hen's friend Ben.
"I have an umbrella."

"Eggs-cellent!" says Hen.

Hen is wet.
Hen's eggs are wet.
"Help!" says Hen.

"You bet!" Ben tells Hen.
"Let's make a shed."

"Eggs-cellent!" says Hen.

Hen is wet.
Hen's eggs are wet.
"Help!" says Hen.

"I will get my net,"
Ben tells Hen.

"Eggs-cellent!" says Hen.

Hen is wet.
Hen's eggs are wet.
"I give up!" says Hen.

"I will never give up,"
Ben tells Hen.

Ben does not give up.
Hen tends her eggs.

Ten wet days go by.

Then twenty.
"It will be wet forever,"
Hen says.
"Nothing lasts forever,"
says Ben.

The next day,
Ben says, "Hen, look!"

Hen says, "Ben, look!"

"Eggs-cellent!" says Ben.
"Ben, you are the best," says Hen.

Story Starters

Ben has a net.
What will Ben get
in his net?

Fred is in bed.
Will you tell Fred
a bedtime story?